10 × 8/10

D0574639

10 × 8/10

GIANT STEPS

By ELIZABETH LOREDO

Illustrated by BARRY ROOT

G. P. PUTNAM'S SONS · NEW YORK

Published simultaneously in Canada. Manufactured in China by South China Printing Co. Ltd.
Designed by Gunta Alexander. Text set in Stempel Schneidler.
The art was done in watercolor, gouache, and pastel pencil
on 140 lb. Arches Hot Press paper.

Library of Congress Cataloging-in-Publication Data
Loredo, Elizabeth. Giant steps / by Elizabeth Loredo ; illustrated by Barry Root.   p. cm.
Summary: Five giants play a global game of tag, and while the first four run just as far
as they can go, north, south, east, and west, the unlucky fifth giant has to count.
[1. Giants—Fiction. 2. Tag games—Fiction.] I. Root, Barry, ill. II. Title.
PZ7.L8787Gi 2004   [E]—dc21   2003005975
ISBN 0-399-23491-8
10 9 8 7 6 5 4 3 2 1
First Impression

To Mom & Dad,
for all the bedtime stories
and your infinite love—E. L.

For Jon Ernest Bulcken—B. R.

Five loud-sighin' giants sittin' on a mountaintop.
Five eye-rollin' giants sittin' on a mountaintop.
Five yawny-bored giants sittin' on a mountaintop,
    all of them wonderin' what they should do.

"Hey, my friends. Let's play giant steps."

So they one potata, two potata, three potata, four.
And they five potata, six potata, seven potata, more.
And that fifth giant, he never is lucky like the rest.
That fifth giant, he is IT.

So while that fifth giant, he slowly starts countin',
  he slowly starts countin' one two three four five . . .

the other giants, they all take off runnin'.

The first giant, he run north
   just as far and as fast as he could go.
He run out over snow-white slopes and bobbing icebergs and
      seals slippin' and swimmin'
         among the slow frozen fish.

The second giant, she run south
    just as far and as fast as she could go.
She run out over wide wavy plains and dark tangle jungles and
        elephants trumpetin' and thumpetin'
            with the wild wildebeest.

The third giant, he run east
  just as far and as fast as he could go.
He run out over jaggy-tip mountains and bottomless pools and
  shaggy sheep roamin' through
  spittin' camel herds.

The fourth giant, she run west
　　just as far and as fast as she could go.
She run out over red-stripe desert and yawn-mouth canyons
　　and thirsty coyote howlin' at scaredy jackrabbits.

So those four giants, they go runnin'.
They go runnin' to the north, south, east and west.
They go runnin' just as far and as fast
as any giant you ever seen.
Until that fifth giant, he finishes up his countin' and he yells.
He yells just as loud and as loud as he could yell.
He yells . . .

FREEZE!

And wherever that yell, it echoes, wherever that yell,
it echoes all over, everywhere—everybody, they just . . .

FROZE!

They froze in the west—
    thirsty coyote,
        scaredy jackrabbits,
           giant and all.

They froze in the east—
    shaggy sheep,
        spittin' camel herd,
           giant and all.

They froze in the south—
    trumpetin' thumpetin' elephants,
    wild wildebeest,
        giant and all.

They froze in the north—
    slippery seals, slow frozen fish,
      giant and all.
            They ESPECIALLY froze in the north.

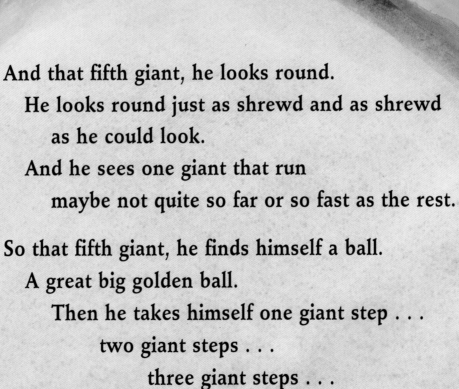

And that fifth giant, he looks round.
   He looks round just as shrewd and as shrewd
      as he could look.
   And he sees one giant that run
      maybe not quite so far or so fast as the rest.

So that fifth giant, he finds himself a ball.
   A great big golden ball.
      Then he takes himself one giant step . . .
            two giant steps . . .
                  three giant steps . . .
And he throws that golden ball
   just as hard as he could throw it.
      Throws it at that one giant who run
            not quite so fast or so far as the rest.

That ball. It misses.

That fifth giant, he never is lucky.
"You're IT," say the four giants as they run back
    from the north, the south, the east and the west.
        Four giants blowin' four big raspberries
            just as noisy and annoyin' as they could blow.

"You're IT. Again."

Then those four giants, they all start snickerin'.
And that fifth giant, he starts snortlin' too.
They ALL start snickerin' and snortlin'
hee-hee-hah-ho-hoo.
Snickerin' themselves fit to bust.

On account of they all know that fifth giant, he never is lucky.
He never is lucky, so that fifth giant, he's IT every time out.

And that's a lucky thing for those giants
to the north, south, east and west.

On account of he's the only giant can COUNT.

One two three four five . . .